Nellie Choc-Ice

and the
Plastic Island

JEREMY STRONG

Nellie Choc-Ice

and the
Plastic Island

Illustrated by
Jamie Smith

Barrington Stoke

First published in 2019 in Great Britain by
Barrington Stoke Ltd
18 Walker Street, Edinburgh, EH3 7LP

www.barringtonstoke.co.uk

Text © 2019 Jeremy Strong
Illustrations © 2019 Jamie Smith

A CIP catalogue record for this book is available
from the British Library upon request

ISBN: 978-1-78112-877-0

Printed in China by Leo

This book is in a super-readable format for young readers
beginning their independent reading journey.

For Isaac and Alexander

– Jamie Smith

Contents

Chapter 1

What is a Macaroni Penguin?

Do you know what a Macaroni Penguin is? Maybe you aren't sure, so here is a picture. They have bright yellow feathers sticking out like giant shaggy eyebrows and they live in the Antarctic, near the South Pole.

There is one Macaroni Penguin who is VERY special. Her name is Nellie Choc-Ice. She is the Most Famous Penguin Explorer In The World. She travelled all the way to the North Pole, in the Arctic Ocean, which is where penguins don't live.

Nellie loves her big family and they love her. Here you can see her parents, Small-Ma and Small-Pa. You can also see Grand-Ma and Grand-Pa, plus lots of uncles, aunts and cousins. Can you see Nellie's uncle? He's the one with a hat who plays the guitar.

Nellie longs to get back to her family but it's a long, long way from the North Pole to the South Pole. (Twelve thousand, four hundred and thirty miles, in fact.)

Luckily, Nellie has made friends with Captain Beardy-Beard, who has a submarine.

He and his crew are taking her back to the South Pole. But at the moment they are stuck in New York harbour. This is because the submarine has had an accident.

You see, the submarine ran out of diesel fuel and Nellie Choc-Ice made a BIG MISTAKE.

She thought she could help by putting lots of fish in the fuel tank. Eating fish gives a penguin lots of energy to keep going. Nellie thought eating fish would give the submarine lots of energy too.

It didn't.

The fish just got stuck in the engine and the submarine stopped working.

Oh dear.

Captain Beardy-Beard was not at all happy.

Luckily, the crew got all the fish out, although it took a very long stinky time.

Then the crew filled the tank with diesel and the submarine was ready to go.

The crew told Nellie that she could press the GO button to start the submarine.

Unluckily, penguins can't read, not even Nellie Choc-Ice. (This is because there are no books or libraries at the South Pole.)

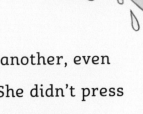

So Nellie made another, even
BIGGER MISTAKE. She didn't press
the GO button. She pressed the
button that said TORPEDOES.

ZAPPPP! A torpedo shot out
of the submarine.

The torpedo went whizzing across the bay and hit the Statue of Liberty. There was a loud bang and the statue's arm fell off. It was the arm holding the flaming torch.

BIGGEST SPLASH EVER! Oh dear, again.

Captain Beardy-Beard was very upset. "Nellie! You—!"

CUP OF
TEA

TORPEDO

GO

REVERS

BISCU

PERISCO

But the captain could only think of rude words to say, so he hid them in his beard where nobody could hear them.

"I think we'd better get out of here, fast," he told the crew.

Chapter 2

The submarine stays underwater

The submarine sailed underwater all week until Captain Beardy-Beard thought it was time to come up to the surface again.

The submarine rose up and up, and just as it broke through the surface there was a terrible grinding noise, the engine grunted to a halt and the submarine stopped dead. Oh dear. (At least this time it wasn't Nellie's fault.)

They all looked at each other in alarm. What had happened?

Captain Beardy-Beard climbed the ladder into the conning tower with Nellie close behind.

The captain opened the hatch slowly and peered out. They were just above the level of the sea. They stared out in horror. Nellie's bright yellow eyebrows went very droopy.

All around the submarine, in every direction, was floating plastic. It came in all sizes, shapes and colours, covered with filthy scum.

The plastic bobbed softly up and down on the waves. The island of plastic stretched as far as the eye could see.

Captain Beardy-Beard rubbed his eyes. "I can't believe it!" he said. "What a filthy, disgusting disaster!"

One by one the crew came up the ladder to take a look. "Oh dear," they all said. (And this time Nellie hadn't even done anything!)

"It's a catastrophe," moaned Nellie. "Now we are stuck in the middle of a disgusting plastic island AND the submarine has broken down. I don't think I shall ever see my family again."

At that moment Nellie spotted something far off, in the middle of the island. It was like a white flag or an arm and it was waving feebly.

"Look! Someone needs our help!" she said. "We must rescue them."

Nellie was right but the captain was worried. "We can't stand on all this wobbly plastic," he told her. "It's not safe. We will fall underwater and get trapped."

"I'll go and see what it is," said Nellie bravely. "It doesn't matter if I fall in, because I'm a penguin and I can swim."

"You be careful, Nellie," warned Captain Beardy-Beard. "Don't take any risks."

Nellie jumped onto the wobbly island. She hopped from one bit of floating plastic to the next.

A few times she almost fell in, but she kept going. That made her feel clever and proud, until she really did fall in and it was horrible.

The plastic was everywhere, trying to pull her down. Nellie was sinking underneath it all. Luckily, Macaroni Penguins can hold their breath for a long time. (About twenty minutes!) Nellie had to work really hard to clamber back on top.

Nellie didn't feel clever any longer. "This plastic disaster is far, far worse than I thought," Nellie muttered to herself.

At last she could see what was waving. It was the wing of a big bird, an albatross. The bird's feet and one wing were caught up in plastic netting. The albatross was thin and hungry. It must have been trapped there for days.

Chapter 3

The bird breaks free

Every so often the albatross tried to break free.

"I'm Nellie. How did you get trapped?" asked Nellie the penguin explorer.

"My name is Toss," the albatross answered. "Friends told me about this plastic island. I flew down to see it for myself and when I landed, my foot got trapped, then the other foot, then one wing. It's awful, horrible. Who threw all this rubbish into the ocean? I've seen hundreds of dead fish. I've even seen a dead whale. The plastic is killing everything."

Nellie pulled and tugged at the twisted netting and the albatross broke free at last, but he was too weak to fly.

"Climb onto my back," said Nellie. "I'll carry you to our submarine."

"What's a submarine?" asked Toss as Nellie plodded step by step towards the distant submarine.

"It's a thing that goes underwater," Nellie explained.

"Like a fish?"

"A very big fish," said Nellie. "But you climb inside it."

"You climb inside a big FISH?!" squawked Toss. "I put big fish inside ME! I don't want to get inside a fish."

"It's LIKE a fish," said Nellie. "But it's a submarine."

"That's what you said at the beginning," the albatross complained. "And I still don't know what a submarine is."

37

Captain Beardy-Beard and the crew
helped Nellie and the albatross onto the
deck. They went inside the submarine.

"This isn't like a fish at all," snapped
the albatross, looking all around.

That annoyed Nellie. "Excuse me, Toss. I just saved your life and now you're complaining. Maybe I should put you back on Plastic Island. I might add that you're very heavy. I shall need a back massage after carrying you all that way."

Then Toss stopped grumbling and said, "Thank you." He held up one big flat paddle foot and said, "Actually, I have very good feet for giving a back massage, if anyone's interested. But first of all I'd like a cup of coffee and a biscuit."

The crew gave Toss some food and afterwards he gave Nellie a nice back massage, and Captain Beardy-Beard too. They talked about what they should do about Plastic Island.

"It's an ocean calamity," said Nellie.
"It stretches for miles. Toss says
that hundreds of animals have been
affected – fish, whales, dolphins, birds."

Toss nodded. "What's even worse is that the island stretches much further than you can see. Plastic, plastic, plastic! What are people doing to the ocean?"

"Well, we can't just pick it all up,"
said the captain. "And we can't go
anywhere yet because the submarine's
propeller is tangled up in it. I can't
send a diver down to sort it out because
the diver might get trapped. I think we
shall be stuck here for ever."

Chapter 4

Nellie has an idea

Nellie had an idea and she jumped up. "I can dive down to the propeller. I can hold my breath for twenty-two and a half minutes."

"I thought it was twenty," Captain Beardy-Beard said.

"I've been practising," said Nellie proudly. "And I've had another idea. When we get to land, we will get the people who make all this disgusting plastic to come out here and clear it all up! Then we shall tell everyone in the world that they MUST STOP USING SO MUCH PLASTIC!"

The crew all cheered when they heard this. It was a good plan from a clever penguin.

Then Nellie swam down through all the layers and layers of plastic rubbish and found the submarine's propeller.

Nearby was a dolphin struggling in some plastic netting. It took Nellie a long time to cut the dolphin free with her beak. She had to come up for air three times but in the end both the submarine and the dolphin were free.

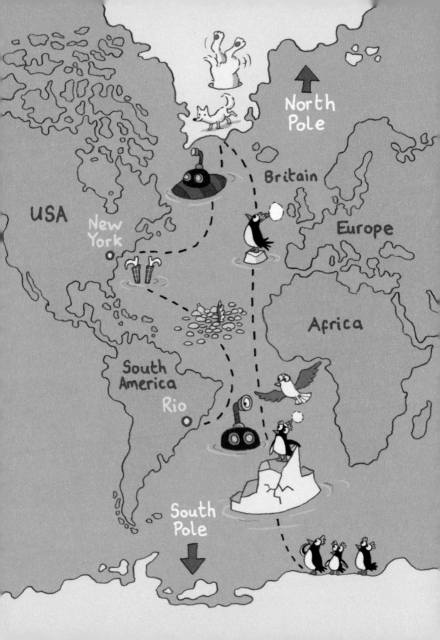

Captain Beardy-Beard carefully took the submarine away from the rubbish and they set off for the nearest land.

Soon they arrived at the capital of Brazil, Rio de Janeiro.

The captain arranged some
VERY IMPORTANT MEETINGS with
some VERY IMPORTANT PEOPLE. They
came from every country in the world
to hear what Captain Beardy-Beard,
Toss and Nellie had to say.

"We MUST clear up the plastic mess," said Captain Beardy-Beard. "It's a problem we must all try to solve. It is killing everything in the oceans."

"It nearly killed me," interrupted Toss.

"And me," added Nellie. "We must get rid of it all and stop using so much plastic."

"If you don't," said Toss, "I shall get all my albatross friends to come and peck your ears."

"And all MY penguin friends will peck your bottoms," Nellie added crossly. "Very hard."

The Very Important People looked at Nellie's and Toss's beaks and they were worried and scared. But how could they get rid of such a gigantic island?

Nellie had to wait for a long time while people argued about how they could clean up the oceans.

It was another long delay for the little penguin. Would she ever see Small-Ma and Small-Pa and all her relations again?

At last the Very Important People worked out how to get rid of Plastic Island.

They built enormous ships. Some had gigantic gobbling mouths that swallowed rubbish. Some had huge nets that scooped up the plastic.

The ships sailed to the island. They worked night and day. Bit by bit they grabbed all the rubbish and took it away.

They rescued hundreds of trapped animals. It took a long time. At last the plastic was all gone. Nellie and everyone there cheered.

All over the world people were told not to throw away their plastic. It would be collected, taken away, recycled and used over and over again.

That news put a big smile on Nellie's beak. She was very happy.

"The oceans will be clean and safe again for all the animals AND people too," she said.

Chapter 5

At last!

"Now you can go home at last, Nellie," smiled Captain Beardy-Beard. "Come on, hop into the submarine and let's go."

The albatross tapped Captain Beardy-Beard's shoulder. "I like the Antarctic. Perhaps you can take me too?"

Captain Beardy-Beard thought hard about this. "I can take you," he told Toss. "But you must promise not to put fish in the submarine's fuel tank or press any red buttons."

Toss was astonished. "Who would do something as stupid as THAT?" he squawked.

Nellie looked at Captain
Beardy-Beard and the captain looked
at her. He smiled and shook his head.

"Oh, it was just something I heard about from somewhere," he said.

Toss pecked a bit of seaweed off one foot.

"Well, it was very silly," the albatross said. "Anyway, thank you for taking me on your submarine. Any time you'd like a back massage, just ask."

So they set off for the Antarctic at last. And all the way there the submarine was followed by whales and dolphins and fish and seabirds.

They were all singing and squeaking and squawking and shouting, "THANK YOU!"

Then one day the submarine rose to the surface. Captain Beardy-Beard opened the hatch. "Nellie Choc-Ice," he said. "Come here. I have something to show you."

So Nellie went on deck and there, right in front of her, were the great icebergs of home, sparkling like giant diamonds.

On top of the icebergs stood a
long, long line of Macaroni Penguins.
They were waving their flipper-wings,
jumping up and down and shouting.

"NELLIE CHOC-ICE! WELCOME
HOME!"

Nellie was so excited she fell
overboard.

She wanted to swim straight across to her family as soon as possible.

But first of all Nellie clambered back on board the submarine.

She had to say "thank you" to the captain. (That is because good manners are important, even when you are a very excited penguin.)

Nellie gave Captain Beardy-Beard
a big hug. The captain smiled and
hugged her back, even though Nellie was
standing on one of his feet and she was
soaking wet from falling in the sea.

Then Nellie shook hands with all
the crew. At last she came to Toss the
albatross. He was crying.

"You saved my life," Toss told her. "And you saved the ocean from the plastic island."

"*We* saved the ocean," Nellie said. "All of us. It's much easier to do things when there are lots of you doing it."

Toss smiled and soared up into the sky. He turned and swooped around overhead. "Thank you, Nellie Choc-Ice!" he squawked.

At last Nellie was free to swim to her family.

What a fuss they made of her! Nellie had never been hugged so much.

"We are so proud of you," Small-Pa told her. "We have heard all about your adventures and Plastic Island. You have been on The News right around the world. You're famous!"

"Now we must have a party," announced Small-Ma.

So they did and all the penguins came.

They danced through the night to wonderful music being played on the guitar by her uncle, the one with the hat.

The stars shone and high above all the colours of the aurora australis danced with them.